D 4/22/10   WLTN

D0401859

NBA

Steve Nash

by John Hareas

SCHOLASTIC INC.

New York   Toronto   London   Auckland   Sydney
Mexico City   New Delhi   Hong Kong   Buenos Aires

To my three Hall of Famers–
Emma, Christopher and Leah
–J.H.

PHOTO CREDITS

All photos are © NBA/Getty images
Front Cover: Jonathan Daniel
D. Clarke Evans (4); Nathaniel S. Butler (6, 16); Jennifer Pottheiser (12); Jed Jacobsohn (13);
Jason Wise (17); Andy Hayt (19); Glenn James (21, 22); Barry Gossage (24); Garrett Ellwood (25);
Noah Graham (27, 30); Rocky Winder (31); Ned Dishman (32)
Photos pages 7, 8, 9 courtesy of the Nash family

ISBN-13: 978-0-545-03411-1
ISBN-10: 0-545-03411-6

12   11   10   9   8   7   6   5   4   3   2   8   9   10   11   12/0

Printed in the U.S.A.
First printing, January 2008
Book Design by Kim Brown

Contents

Meet Steve Nash

Basketball is not necessarily a game of size and strength. You don't have to be the tallest player or even the biggest to succeed in basketball. How do we know this? Look at Steve Nash, the two-time NBA MVP of the Phoenix Suns.

While the average NBA player is listed at 6-foot-6 and weighs 225 pounds, Steve is 6-foot-3 and 180 pounds. Barely. And Steve is not the fastest player in the NBA. He doesn't have to be. Why? Because he is one of the smartest.

So, how does Steve do it? How does he dominate a sport that features bigger and faster players? Steve is one of the best guards in the NBA because he outthinks his opponents and works very hard every day in practice and in games. Oh, and he also happens to be one of the most creative passers in NBA history.

Left hand, right hand, one-handed passes, it doesn't matter. Steve will always deliver

the ball exactly where it is supposed to go, every time. Steve's teammates are always on the lookout for one of his passes, too. They have to be. Otherwise they just might get a ball in the face!

Steve isn't just a great passer, he's also a creative jump shooter. He shoots what is called a lean-back jumper. Steve will shoot the ball while leaning back, moving away from his opponent. By doing this, he creates space away from his defender.

Since Steve joined the Suns in 2004, Phoenix has led the league in scoring. Thanks to Steve, the Suns play a fast, up-tempo game. If the Suns are a turbo-charged car, then Steve is the engine that makes them go.

Stephen John Nash was born on February 7, 1974 in Johannesburg, South Africa. Steve's dad, John, was a professional soccer player in England and Johannesburg. His mom, Jean, played on England's national netball team. (Netball is a game similar to basketball.) When Steve was just 18 months old, his family moved to Regina, Canada, and then later to Vancouver.

Growing up, Steve was not interested in basketball right away. He was too busy playing other sports such as ice hockey, lacrosse,

soccer, rugby, and baseball. Steve excelled in all of them. Steve also liked to play chess. In elementary school, he was so good that he won three chess titles. His ability to strategize under pressure no doubt served him when on the basketball court, where decisions are made within a split second, especially when you're a point guard like Steve.

Also, like any other kid, Steve had hobbies. One of Steve's hobbies was collecting trading cards.

"I used to collect hockey cards," said Steve. "It was like Vegas at my school. You'd go to school with your box of cards, and at recess and lunchtime there were all these games we'd play."

When Steve wasn't playing sports or collecting cards, he was doing chores at his house.

"I used to have to cut the lawn, and when I

was in junior high school, I worked at a concession stand at a stadium."

It wasn't until junior high that Steve started to get serious about basketball.

"I didn't play basketball until eighth grade," said Steve. "I think a lot of it is because my parents are from London, England, so I played all the other sports my parents introduced me to. When I started playing basketball, I fell in love with it."

"I would shoot in the dark, I would shoot in the rain," said Steve. When Steve wasn't playing, he was watching college and NBA games on TV. He dreamed of playing for a college in the United States. He even told his mom that one day he would play in the NBA.

Steve would have to take the long road to

fulfill his dream though. His first high school coach didn't think he had what it takes to play at the collegiate level. Plus, Steve's grades weren't as good as they needed to be. So, he transferred to St. Michael's University School. Steve improved his grades and soon became a top player. He even led his senior team to the championship.

Even though Steve was a great player, nobody outside of Canada had heard of this dynamic point guard. He was an unknown to the U.S. colleges. Still, Steve wasn't about to give up his dream.

Hello, Santa Clara

Steve dreamed of playing for a top U.S. basketball school. Syracuse. Duke. UCLA. Steve wrote to all of the major schools, hoping to earn a basketball scholarship. While some schools wrote back, none of them were interested in Steve as a basketball player.

"I always had dreams of playing big-time college basketball," said Steve. "Unfortunately, I wouldn't get any recruitment by colleges except Santa Clara."

Santa Clara University, located in the Bay Area of California, was not exactly known as a basketball powerhouse.

"Santa Clara was the only college that actually called us and said send them a tape," said Steve's father John.

The head coach, Dick Davey, was impressed with what he saw of Steve on tape. He traveled up to British Columbia to watch Steve play in

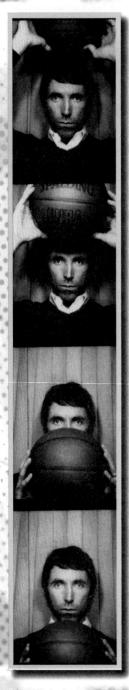

a tournament. Steve starred in the game, making play after play. Davey was impressed with the point guard that no one in the U.S. seemed to be paying attention to. But Davey was also worried. What would happen if another college saw Steve play this well? They would be interested in signing him. Davey looked around the gym and didn't notice anyone from a U.S. college. As luck would have it, Davey was the only U.S. college coach to watch Steve play that day. And Santa Clara was the only college to offer Steve a basketball scholarship.

Steve enrolled at Santa Clara in the summer of 1992. Even before his college career began, his coach told him that his defense was "terrible," and that Steve would have to work on it if he expected to play.

So Steve worked on his defense and his all-around game before the season began. He would shoot in the gym some-times until 3 in the morning. And when school started, Steve even dribbled a tennis ball around campus between classes to help perfect his ballhandling.

Steve started out his freshman season as number 11, the same number as Isiah Thomas, the former Detroit Piston point guard great and one of Steve's basketball idols. Like Thomas, Steve dreamed big and wasn't afraid to reach for the high standards set by basketball greats before him.

Playing at Santa Clara gave Steve the opportunity to get noticed. Steve immediately took charge of his team, showing confidence in himself and in his teammates, and Santa Clara started winning games. At the end of the season, when Steve helped lead the Santa Clara Broncos to the NCAA Tournament, some thought he might transfer to a bigger name school in order to get more attention. But Steve was loyal to Santa Clara and his teammates.

During the next two years, Steve went on to lead the Broncos to upsets of bigger name schools such as UCLA, Michigan State, and Oregon State. He also led the Broncos to two more NCAA Tournaments. Steve earned West Coast Conference Player of the Year honors during his senior season. Steve was finally making a name for himself in the world of college basketball and starting to catch the interest of some NBA teams.

NBA scouts thought that Steve could be a first-round pick. In 1996, other point guards such as Allen Iverson of Georgetown and

Stephon Marbury of Georgia Tech were well known. Since they played at bigger schools, they were on national TV all of the time. But even though Steve played well in college, he would have to prove himself all over again at the NBA level.

To the NBA

Steve was successful at Santa Clara, but he was still relatively overlooked. It wasn't until after his senior year, when he played in a Nike Desert Classic tournament and made the all-tournament team, that NBA teams really took notice.

Still, the questions remained with Steve: Did he have the quickness to compete against

the other quicker and stronger NBA point guards? Was he going to be overmatched on defense?

Many NBA scouts and coaches said Steve reminded them a little bit of one of the all-time greats, John Stockton of the Utah Jazz.

The talk leading up to the NBA Draft was that Steve might get selected in the middle of the first round. In the 1996 Draft, there were 29 NBA teams in the first round. Sure enough, Steve was drafted by the Phoenix Suns with the 15th overall pick.

His dream finally came true.

"I'm just going to try to work just as hard as I can every day from now to the rest of my life," said Steve. "I don't know what else to say. It's a dream come true. It's unbelievable. It's beyond words."

Steve was happy. Too bad the Suns fans weren't. They had wanted Syracuse forward John Wallace, who had been getting a lot of media attention at the time for his performance in the 1996 NCAA Championship game. By contrast, Santa Clara games were barely televised nationally, so Steve Nash was almost a stranger! At a Phoenix draft party, the Suns fans booed Steve's selection.

The boos didn't bother Steve — he wouldn't let them. He was determined to turn them into cheers. "It's a great city and I can't wait to change their opinion," said Steve.

Steve didn't get a chance to play much his rookie season. He averaged 10.5 minutes per game, 3.3 points, and 2.1 assists. Instead he watched and learned behind fellow Suns point guards Kevin Johnson and Jason Kidd.

But in his second season Steve was making strides. He saw his numbers jump to 21.9 minutes per game, 9.1 points, and 3.4 assists.

Steve had the skills to make his mark in the NBA. He just wouldn't get a chance to showcase them in Phoenix.

Growing Pains in Big D

S teve's big break came at the end of his second season. Since the Suns were loaded at the point guard position, they traded Steve to the Dallas Mavericks on June 24, 1998, the day of the Draft. The Mavericks were excited to have Steve on their team. Mavs coach, Don Nelson, used to coach the Golden State Warriors, another California team, and remembered Steve from his Santa Clara days. Nelson was familiar with Steve's game and liked what he had seen. The Mavs showed its faith in Steve by signing him to a contract extension.

But the Mavericks weren't finished on Draft Day. They also

traded their first round pick — Robert "Tractor" Traylor to Milwaukee for their first round pick, a 7-foot German forward named Dirk Nowitzki. Two bold moves by the Mavs on the same day. The fans and the team were excited. But things didn't go so well in that first season.

As talented as Steve and Dirk were, they experienced growing pains together as the team struggled in their first season. Dirk was still getting used to living in America for the first time and the fast pace and physical nature of the NBA game. Steve wasn't producing on the court as well and the fans didn't hide their disappointment. Steve realized that it was a big difference to go from coming off the bench in Phoenix to being the starting point guard in Dallas.

"They booed him in our own gym every time he touched the ball," said Dirk. "I remember sitting on the floor, like, 'Wow, this is pretty messed up.'"

Steve and Dirk may have struggled on the court but at least they had each other to lean on off the court. Both players were adjusting to a new city and ended up living in the same apartment complex. As a result, they hung out a lot.

"We really didn't know anyone else," said Steve.

"[Steve] became my best friend here immediately," said Dirk. "I was homesick, always calling home to Germany. And Steve was the first one who made me feel really welcome here."

Steve and Dirk used their friendship bond to help strengthen their games. They would always encourage each other as they continued to develop as basketball players. They pushed each other to reach new heights.

"We were constantly working on our games

together and kind of grew together," said Dirk.

In 2001, everything started to come together for Steve, Dirk, and the Mavs. Steve emerged as the team's fiery leader and Dirk as his wing man. They were soon becoming one of the NBA's top one-two combos.

Steve and Dirk helped end the Mavs' 11-year playoff drought. The Mavs would advance to the Western Conference Semifinals in back-to-back years. In the 2003 Western Conference Finals, the Mavs advanced only to lose in six games to the eventual NBA champions, the San Antonio Spurs. In the process of the team's success, Steve and Dirk became NBA All-Stars.

While the future looked bright for Steve, Dirk, and the Mavs, everything changed in the summer of 2004. They would no longer be teammates.

Hello Again, Phoenix

Steve was a free agent during the Summer of 2004. He thought for sure he would re-sign with the Mavericks and continue to lead the team's climb toward a championship. When the 2003–04 season ended, Steve received a better, longer-term offer from the Suns, than what the Mavs had offered him. When Steve gave Dallas a chance to match, they didn't, but Steve couldn't imagine playing for another team.

"It hurt to not to be wanted back," said Steve. "I thought we were going to play our careers out in

Dallas and win a championship. In many ways we were left thinking what could have been."

As surprised as Steve was, he didn't look back. There wasn't any time. He now needed to figure out ways to improve a team that had won only 29 games. At the age of 30, when most point guards were on the down side of their careers, Steve raised his game to new heights and took the Suns along for a ride that season.

Steve led the Suns to an amazing turnaround, winning 62 games in his first season. Steve also directed the league's most exciting offense, thanks to head coach Mike D'Antoni's Run and Gun offensive philosophy — which meant pushing the ball up and down the court at a fast pace. The Suns were not only scoring with this method, but were winning many fans who loved watching this style of play.

Even though Steve finished the 2004–05 season fourth on his team in scoring with only 15.5 points, he averaged a career high of 11.5 assists per game. He was rewarded for his unselfish play with the NBA's MVP award.

Steve became the first Canadian to win the award, and like the unselfish player that he is, Steve made sure every one of his teammates

joined him at the podium for his acceptance speech.

In the 2005 Playoffs, the Suns faced the Mavs in the Western Conference Semifinals. It was Steve and Dirk in the playoffs once again but now on opposite sides.

"It's a strange situation to play Dallas in the playoffs," said Steve who had spent a total of four seasons in Dallas.

It was equally strange for Dirk who really missed his buddy Steve.

"It was pretty tough to see how well he was playing for Phoenix," said Dirk. "We were all kind of wishing he was still here. It was weird to see him in a different uniform."

Steve starred in that series, dominating the Mavs with clutch baskets while getting his teammates involved. The Suns won the series in six games.

"I've never seen him play better than this," said Dirk after the series. "I think he wanted to show all of Dallas what we missed and he did that."

All-Time Great

The second go-around in Phoenix couldn't have been any better for Steve. He turned around the team's reputation in the league overnight. Proving that his first return season in Phoenix wasn't a fluke, Steve was on a mission once again. Under Steve's leadership, he led the Suns to 54 wins and again won NBA MVP honors. It was his second straight award! Steve joined Hall of Famer Magic Johnson as the only point guards in NBA history to win two awards. Steve also became one of only nine players to win the award in consecutive seasons.

Steve also averaged 10.5 assists per game and was responsible for six of his teammates averaging career highs.

In Steve's third season with the Suns in 2006–07, he led the team to 61 victories and once again his team was No. 1 in scoring. It was the sixth straight season a Steve Nash-led team led the league in scoring.

Steve almost won his third NBA MVP in a row! He fell short to his friend Dirk Nowitzki who won it for the first time and Steve couldn't be happier.

Steve is known as the ultimate leader and team player both on and off the court. He is involved in several charities around the world. In British Columbia, Canada, the Steve Nash youth basketball league features more than 8,000 players and 850 teams based all over the province.

In 2001, he created the Steve Nash Foundation, which helps urban youth. In Toronto, he is raising money to build an all-access, all kids community center. Steve also donated all of his endorsement money in 2006 to a hospital in Asuncion, Paraguay, to help open a new intensive care unit for kids who don't have access to quality health care in the area. This hospital project is especially close to Steve's heart since it's in the same city where his wife grew up.

Steve's work has not gone unnoticed. In 2006, Time Magazine honored Steve in their "100 People Who Shape Our World" issue. In that special issue, Hall of Famer Charles Barkley wrote about Steve and how impressed the basketball great was with Steve's generosity. "What has [Steve] taught us? It pays to be selfless. You can be content just to make the players around you better. . . . Over the past few years, his popularity has exploded. His ego could have swelled — everyone else's does. But he still just wants to pass the ball."